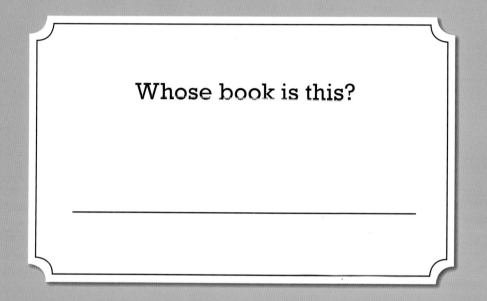

Whose book is this?

_____

CHLOE
and the
LION

MAC BARNETT
Pictures by ADAM REX

Disney • HYPERION

LOS ANGELES   NEW YORK

First Edition, April 2012
10 9 8 7 6 5
FAC-029191-18018
Printed in Malaysia

Library of Congress Cataloging-in-Publication Data

Barnett, Mac.
  Chloe and the lion / Mac Barnett ; pictures by Adam Rex. — 1st ed.
     p. cm.
  Summary: Mac, the author, fires Adam, the illustrator, over their
artistic differences about Chloe, the main character of their book,
until Mac realizes both of their talents are needed and they must work
together or their story about Chloe will never be finished.
  ISBN 978-1-4231-1334-8 (Reinforced bdg.)
  [1. Authorship—Fiction. 2. Cooperativeness—Fiction. 3. Humorous
stories.] I. Rex, Adam, ill. II. Title.
  PZ7.B26615Ch 2012
  [Fic]—dc22   2011006561

The art in this book was made with basswood, balsa wood, oil and
acrylic paints, pencil, Sculpey clay, modified doll clothing, toilet
paper, photography, and Photoshop.

Designed by Tyler Nevins

Text is set in Rockwell Std, Century Schoolbook Std/Monotype;
Adobe Garamond Pro/Fontspring

Hand lettering by Adam Rex

Reinforced binding

Visit www.DisneyBooks.com

CHLOE
and the
LION

This is me, Mac.
I'm the author of this book.

To Adam Rex

　　　　　　　　—M.B.

For Jennifer, who's dealing
with a lot of lions lately.

　　　　　　　　—A.R.

This is my friend,
Adam.
He's the illustrator
of this book.

And this is Chloe.
She's the main character of this book.

Wherever Chloe went, she looked for loose change.

She would find nickels on sidewalks, dimes under couches, and quarters in pinball machines.

All week long, Chloe would save the money she found in a glass jar.

Then, on Saturday, she would walk from her house, through the forest, and over to the park, where she would buy a ticket to ride the merry-go-round.

But one week, Chloe found a lot of change.

So she was able to buy a lot of tickets.

And she rode around and around and around.

Which was why she got very dizzy.

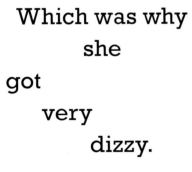

And that's how Chloe ended up lost in the forest.

It was getting dark, and the forest was filled with noises. And just as Chloe realized she'd been walking in circles,

a huge **lion** leapt out
from behind an oak tree.

I'm sorry.
Hold on.

Adam, could you come out here?

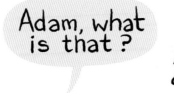

Suddenly, an artist walked into the clearing, carrying paintbrushes and all the other stuff he'd need to illustrate a **brilliant** story written by a **true genius**.

This is me, Mac.
I'm the author
of this book.

This is my new
friend, Hank.
He's the illustrator
of this book.

And this is Chloe, the main
character of this book,
who has just been surprised
by a huge lion.

The first thing the lion did was walk
up to Adam and swallow him whole.

Then the beast turned to Chloe and let out a noisy roar.

I'm sorry. Hold on.

I give up.

And this is Chloe.

Wait— no, this is Chloe.

No, that's not right. I think Adam drew her like this.

No.

No! No! No!

Who am I kidding?

This book is a disaster.

Look, Hank. This isn't working out.

YOU'RE NOT GOING TO HAVE THE LION EAT ME, ARE YOU?

Just go.

This is me, Mac. I'm the author **and** illustrator of this book.

"But so what? You're the writer. Adam is the illustrator. We all add something to the story."

"But you can't just stop telling it."

Hello?

Adam, I was wrong. Hank's not as good as you are and I'm terrible at drawing and... Well, this book needs both of us. I want you to draw the pictures.

Anything else?

I couldn't quite read that.

I'm sorry.

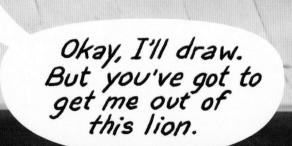

This is me, Mac.
I'm the author of this book.

This is my friend, Adam.
He's the illustrator of this book.

She followed the footprints right up to a cave in the side of a mountain. Terrifying roars and horrible smells came blasting from its entrance.

"Lion! I am Chloe! Come and meet your match!"

Clearly, the knight was an idiot. So Chloe went on alone.

Chloe had a plan.

She heard the sound of metal grinding on metal, and she stumbled upon a knight. Before she could even start talking, the knight began:

"Hail there, girl. I am a noble knight looking for a quest, and thou art clearly a damsel in distress.

I am ready to help vanquish any foe."

"Great!" said Chloe. "My friend has been swallowed whole by a lion."

"A lion?" asked the knight. "Really? A dragon would be so much cooler."

"My friend has been swallowed by a lion and I'm off to save him," Chloe said.
"Will you help me, farmer?"

"Sorry," said the woman. "I just go after monsters who've been emotionally wounded by their mad-genius creators."

So Chloe went on.

So Chloe went on.
Soon she came across a
knobby crone shoveling
hay with a mean-looking
pitchfork.

And this is Chloe, the world-famous lion hunter.

Chloe followed the trail of paw prints through the forest, and came across a lumberjack felling trees in a clearing.

"My friend has been swallowed by a lion and I'm off to save him," Chloe said. "Will you help me, woodcutter?"

"Nah," said the woodcutter. "I only go after wolves dressed as old ladies."

Chloe could hear the lion's footsteps getting

closer and closer.

They started out thunderous

and grew to be earsplitting.

The footsteps stopped, and Chloe knew

the lion was ready to pounce.

She wondered
whether she
had made a
big mistake.

"I look terrible!" said the lion. "Who drew me?"

"Mac did," said Chloe. "I asked him to."

"How could you let him pick up a pencil? He's **awful!** What a mess! The man should be in artist prison!" The lion went on and on, maybe overreacting a little.

"I am not overreacting," he continued. "Oh! I am **ruined.** And once I was so beautiful!"

And then the lion began to cry.

Chloe saw her chance.

"The only person who can draw you the right way is trapped inside your belly. He's not going to help you out unless you cough him up."

So the lion coughed up Adam.

THE END

"Um, guys?"

"Is that it? I mean, I faced a lion, saved Adam, kept Mac from abandoning the whole story midway through. And this is it?"

"This is how you say thanks?
This is the end?"

And then the lion coughed up a shiny nickel.

THE END.

Then the lion
shook
and the
lion
rumbled
and the lion
wheezed,

and, to everyone's surprise, coughed up a tall,
shiny pile of quarters, nickels, and dimes.

"Um, guys?"

"Is that it? I mean, I faced a lion, saved Adam, kept Mac from abandoning the whole story midway through. And this is it?"

"This is how you say thanks?
This is the end?"

And then the lion coughed up a shiny nickel.

THE END.

Then the lion
shook

and the
lion
rumbled

and the lion
wheezed,

and, to everyone's surprise, coughed up a tall,
shiny pile of quarters, nickels, and dimes.

Exactly enough to buy everyone a ticket for the merry-go-round.